Once
When the World
Was Green

Jan Wahl

ILLUSTRATED BY
Fabricio Vandenbroeck

TRICYCLE PRESS
Berkeley, California

A Note on the Source of *Once When the World Was Green*

This is a made-up story. It began one lazy afternoon when I lay under a magic jacaranda tree outside my house in central Mexico. Beside me was a copy of the *Popol Vuh*, the "bible" of the Mayan people, that tells of the dawn of life. Nobody knows when that wonderful book was written, or first told. *Once When the World Was Green* is faithful to symbols and themes of the *Popol Vuh*. I began to imagine a Mayan kind of first family. Of course, corn is, and always has been, the most important food crop in Mexico and that is why I call the central character Corn Grower. A long visit to the Yucatan region of Mexico, the home of the Maya, further inspired me. The paintings in this book reflect animals and geography found around La Ruta Maya—that area near Belize, Guatemala, and the Yucatan. I am grateful to Fabricio Vandenbroeck for sharing his knowledge and travels to make our fable as authentic as possible.   —JAN WAHL

TRICYCLE PRESS
P.O. Box 7123
Berkeley, California 94707

Text design by Nancy Austin
Cover design by Nancy Austin and Fabricio Vandenbroeck

Library of Congress Cataloging-in-Publication Data
Wahl, Jan.
    Once when the world was green / Jan Wahl / illustrations, Fabricio Vandenbroeck.
        p.   cm.
    Summary: When his vanity and greed cause him to needlessly kill animals, Corn
Grower almost loses his precious life with his wife, Moon-Sun, and their son, Small Ears.
    ISBN 1-883672-12-0
    [1. Mayas—Fiction. 2. Indians of Central America—Fiction.
  3. Human-animal relationships—Fiction.] I. Vandenbroeck, Fabricio, 1954– ill. II. Title.
PZ7.W12660n 1996
[Fic]—dc20   94-49534
                                            CIP
                                           AC

First Tricycle Press printing, 1996

Manufactured in Singapore

1 2 3 4 5 6 — 00 99 98 97 96

For Douglas and Ilse
with love

— *JW*

For Nadia, Carlo, and Fabio
with love

— *FVB*

Once humans lived with beasts of the
earth and fish of the sea and birds of the air
in perfect harmony.

The world lay green and a Great Tree stood
in full bloom.

One evening, at dusk, a warm
wind blew. Corn Grower was
done with his hoe in the cornfield.
Moon-Sun, his wife, made tasty
tortillas.

　　After they ate they sat with
Small Ears, their baby boy.
Moon-Sun blew on a bamboo flute
and sang the song of life.

Softly, Corn Grower beat upon a
little tree-trunk drum. Flowers from the
tree swayed overhead. There was a
noise from a passing bird. Moon-Sun
stopped strumming. "Is it our child,
learning to speak?"

Corn Grower laughed. "Only a silly
macaw, nothing more."

The vast sky turned purple-orange as the
great setting sun sank behind a dim mountain.

"Soon Small Ears will be too big to carry,"
Moon-Sun said. Mother and father gave the boy
a kiss good night and lay on their straw pallet
and slept.

In the morning, Moon-Sun ground corn into
meal and Corn Grower left the hut for the field.
He saw the glorious fur of a coati who dug near-
by. He saw the bright plumage of a quetzal on the
hut's roof.

He leaned upon his hoe, thinking hard. "Why
do they have fur and feathers—and I do not?"

Quickly, he made a bow and arrow from
a young branch and sharp flint. He shot the coati
and quetzal. From them he fashioned a fine cloak.

Proudly, he showed it to his wife, who shook her head
in horror. "You are warm enough already."

Corn Grower was eager to know what he looked like.
So he walked away to gaze into the stream. "Take the water
jug with you," Moon-Sun called out. He did not hear.

Moon-Sun dug graves and put flowers on the quetzal
and coati. She bent her head silently.

Leaning over the cold blue stream, Corn Grower
watched a slow turtle. "That brilliant shell will make
an amulet to go with my cloak." And so he slew the turtle.

Watching
Corn Grower from
the sky was the wise
Lord of Eagles. He dipped,
gliding low under the rim of
white clouds, then flew off toward
a misty mountain. "Come and see,"
he screeched to his brothers. A band
of eagles circled over Corn Grower, who
strutted and preened foolishly in fur,
feathers, and shell.

"He killed our cousin Quetzal."

That afternoon, Corn Grower sat with his wife and son by the Great Tree. Small Ears lay on his straw mat, kicking and cooing. Sadly Moon-Sun played on her flute. A lazy armadillo shuffled beside them.

"I have nothing but a poor drum," Corn Grower sighed. "I could make a wonderful guitar out of that," and with a club he slew the armadillo.

Moon-Sun shuddered at what her husband did.
"We have music enough," she said, turning away.

"Horrible!" cawed the Lord of Eagles, who was
keeping a sharp eye on the family. Swiftly he picked
up the baby Small Ears from under the tree.

Off flew the Lord of Eagles. He and
Lady Eagle decided they must raise the
child themselves.

Corn Grower picked up a stone and
flung it high as he could. Moon-Sun
screamed as her son disappeared in the
sky. "Now we are punished for those
deeds you did," she cried.

Her husband shook an angry fist.
"I will find our son," he promised,
"no matter how far I must go!"

That same day, he donned a jaguar
mask made from corn paste. "Those birds
won't know who I am. All will fear me."
And he caught a wild tapir and rode it
away in search of his lost son.

Moon-Sun built a fire of sticks and waited by the Great Tree that night and many nights after. A kind owl kept her company and brought a brown mouse to share, but she had no appetite.

On rushed Corn Grower riding the tapir through the
jungle into deep, dark night.

Here and there, moonrays blazed down through green,
high, lush leaves. Parrots squawked. Quick deer dashed
by and lizards crawled. Mosquitoes buzzed. To each
as he passed, he wailed: "Oh! WHERE
is my son?"

Corn Grower remembered evenings
spent with Moon-Sun and Small Ears
under the blooming tree. How he
wished he were there with them.

A real jaguar stared at him and
was not fooled. He flung off his mask,
ashamed.

The turtle shell amulet began to feel heavy. Soon he flung it off and tossed it into the grass. The fur and feather cloak was hot and thick and itchy. He flung it off and rode on.

He encountered a monkey family. The parents each carried a baby who clung tightly. The father monkey stopped to stare.

"We know about you," said the father. "How your son was taken."

"Why can I understand you?" Corn Grower asked.

"Because you are listening," replied the monkey.

Corn Grower leaned down so the two were eye to eye.

"Eagles live on the tallest mountain peak," the monkey added. "You cannot climb there."

"But I won't go home without him," wailed the man as the family left him behind.

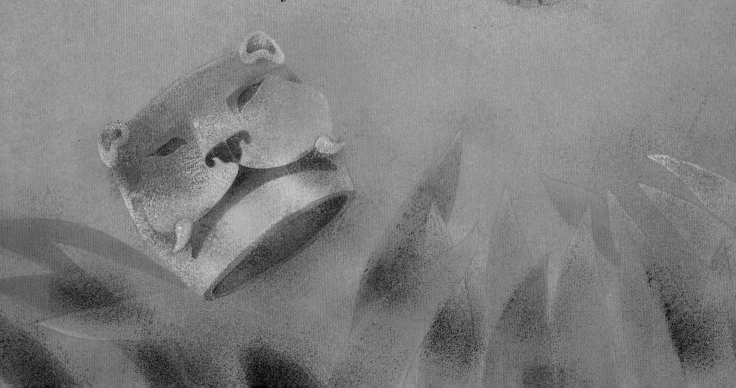

On, on he rode until the night itself vanished and it was cool, pink, damp dawn. He entered a valley sweet with vanilla. Corn Grower climbed off the tapir to stretch his legs, then lay on the grass and dozed wearily. When he awoke the tapir had gone. He was alone.

Suddenly a torrent of rain hurled down and a strong wind roared. Jagged bolts of lightning split the sky. It was day but the sky was pitch black!

Corn Grower struggled to his feet. Wild water washed his hair which had grown long. He had no idea how many weeks he had wandered.

The storm lifted. He leaped for safety as scorpions and snakes scuttled in his path. "Moon-Sun was right. I am being punished."

He turned back, somehow stumbling homeward.
Under the Great Tree, Moon-Sun was waiting. The tree
lay bare and dry, as naked and thin as Corn Grower.
Bats instead of blooms slept on its branches.

Moon-Sun had not been able to tend to everything.
The cornfield was filled with ants. The tiny hut was falling
apart. Moon-Sun whispered, "Where is our son?" Corn
Grower shook his head in despair and held her. He sobbed
and did not reply.

Day turned to dusk and the quiet south wind blew. A rabbit who was not afraid hopped forward. Softly, the man and woman stroked its soft fur. Soft as the hair of their lost son.

Meanwhile on the mountain, Small Ears grew, but could not fly.

Lady Eagle hissed. "This one will never be ours. We must push it from our nest. Look, no wings sprout. He cannot utter our sounds. And he is too big!"

Reluctantly, the Lord of Eagles agreed and hoped that the humans could raise the child better.

They lifted him and off they flew, his toes dangling in air. Small Ears saw the whole huge, dazzling landscape that an eagle sees. For hours they carried the boy until they heard the pitiful noises of human crying.

Underneath the tree, Moon-Sun and Corn Grower
wept. She was trimming his tangled hair and he looked
up and saw their son.

Now, the eagles knew Small Ears
belonged on earth. Gently they laid him
at the feet of his parents. Then they
sailed into the sunny sky waving their
wings in farewell. With a clatter,
sleeping bats awoke, fluttering from
a bare tree.

"Mamá, Papá!" the boy cried his
first words and in an instant the Great
Tree burst into blooms of every color
from the rainbow. Moon-Sun wrapped
her shawl about him like a leaf
round a lily.

Small Ears, who was tired, slept. Both parents
cuddled him in their laps until the first stars rang out
like crystals in a silver breeze.

Birds and deer and others gathered as the father
beat a lullaby on a little tree-trunk drum and the
mother played an evening flute.